Funny Bone Readers™

Being Yourself

Go, Billy, Go!

by Wiley Blevins • illustrated by John Gordon

RED
CHAIR
•PRESS•

Please visit our website at **www.redchairpress.com**.
Find a free catalog of all our high-quality products for young readers.

This book is dedicated to the memory of
Ronin Shimizu, Folsom, CA.

Publisher's Cataloging-In-Publication Data
(Prepared by The Donohue Group, Inc.)

Blevins, Wiley.
    Go, Billy, go! : being yourself / by Wiley Blevins ; illustrated by John Gordon.
-- [First edition].

    pages : illustrations ; cm. -- (Funny bone readers. Dealing with bullies)

    Summary: Billy is a typical boy who loves to ride his bike and play video games.
But when Billy tells his family and friends he wants to be a cheerleader, everyone is
surprised and starts taunting him. But Billy practices and practices and when he shows
his skills at the big game, everyone is impressed and becomes proud of him. Includes
glossary, as well as questions to self-check comprehension.
    Interest age level: 004-008.
    Edition statement supplied by publisher.
    Issued also as an ebook.
    ISBN: 978-1-63440-003-9 (library hardcover)
    ISBN: 978-1-63440-004-6 (paperback)

    1. Boys--Juvenile fiction. 2. Cheerleading--Juvenile fiction. 3. Bullying--Juvenile
fiction. 4. Self-confidence in children--Juvenile fiction. 5. Sex role in children--Juvenile
fiction. 6. Boys--Fiction. 7. Cheerleading--Fiction. 8. Bullying--Fiction.
9. Self-confidence--Fiction. 10. Sex role--Fiction. I. Gordon, John, 1952 Jan 12- II. Title.

PZ7.B618652 Go 2015
[E]   2014958270

This series first published by:
Red Chair Press LLC   PO Box 333   South Egremont, MA 01258-0333

Printed in the United States of America

042015 1P WRZF15

Billy is a boy.

He wears pants.
He rides a big, red bike.

And he plays video games.

But there is one thing different about Billy.

Billy wants to be a cheerleader.

7

Billy was more than sure.
He could do a cartwheel.

He could even do a backward flip!

He could jump high in the air.

He could smile really big
and yell really loud.

So, Billy told the kids at school.
And they all laughed.

But Billy really wanted to be
a cheerleader.
So he closed his ears
and held his head high.
And he practiced and he practiced
and he practiced.

Finally, the day of the big game came.

A group of kids stood up.
"Look at Billy!" they yelled and laughed.

Billy did his cartwheel.
The crowd looked at Billy.

Billy jumped higher in the air
than anyone else.
The crowd whispered.

Billy smiled really big
and yelled really loud.
The crowd stood up and . . .

. . . clapped and clapped and clapped.

19

20

21

Billy is a boy.
He wears pants.
He rides a big, red bike.
And he plays video games.
But more than anything else . . .

Billy is a cheerleader.
Go, Billy, Go!

Big Questions: At first Billy's friends laughed at him. How do you think they felt at the end of the story? How do you know? Have you ever wanted to do something your friends thought was silly? How did you feel?

Big Words:

cheerleader: a person in a group who leads a crowd to support a team

practiced: to learn by doing something